THAT BEAR CAN'T BABYSIT

Caspar Clive Dottie

Ruth Quayle
Alison Friend

nosy crow

Mr and Mrs Burrow had an awful lot of children.
There was Anna and Adelaide, Betsy and Bill, Caspar and Clive,
and, of course, there was little Dottie, too.

Most of the time they muddled along quite nicely, but last
Friday an invitation arrived and, well, things got a bit tricky.

"Oooh!" said Mrs Burrow. "A party!"
Then she looked at her children.
"Oh dear," she said. "We can't possibly go."

"We can," said Mr Burrow. "We'll get a babysitter."

BABYSITTER
WANTED
FOR 7
BUNNIES

But nobody called.
Nobody knocked.
Nobody queued up outside.
Well, nobody except . . .

. . . Bear.

Bear did not have a smart suit.
He did not have shiny shoes.
And he was a bit . . . dreamy.

"That Bear can't babysit,"
gulped Mrs Burrow.

But they were going to be late
for the party.

So they flung on their best
clothes, and Mrs Burrow crossed
her fingers and waved goodbye.

"What shall we do?" said Bear.
"Shall I read you a story?"

"Actually," said Anna politely, "we can read
by ourselves. We like to read scary stories."

"Are you sure you're allowed?" asked Bear.

Adelaide smiled. "Oh yes. Mum and Dad always let us read *The Bunny Beast*."

"Really?" said Bear.

"Yes, **always**," said Anna and Adelaide, winking at each other.

"Once in a dark forest lived the Bunny Beast," whispered Adelaide. "He hid behind trees and waited for baby rabbits to hop past. Then, he sharpened his claws . . ."

The bunnies were scared. They pulled their ears over their eyes. And Anna and Adelaide began to cry.
"We shouldn't be reading this book," wailed Anna and Adelaide.

"That Bear can't babysit!"

"Oh dear," said Bear. "Perhaps we need something to eat?"

"We'll cook," said Betsy.

"Are you sure you're allowed?" asked Bear.

"Oh yes," said Bill. "Mum and Dad always let us make supper."

"Really?" said Bear.

"Yes, always," said Betsy and Bill, winking at each other.

Betsy and Bill prepared
a yummy supper of
178 sweets, 7 helpings
of ice cream, 36 biscuits and
a big jar of chocolate spread.

They all felt **very** sick.

"We shouldn't be eating this food," sobbed Betsy and Bill.

"That Bear can't babysit!"

"Oh dear," said Bear. "Perhaps a spot of fresh air would make you feel better?"

But Caspar and Clive ran straight for the hosepipe.

"Are you sure you're allowed to do that?" Bear asked.

"Oh yes," said Caspar, nudging Clive. "Mum and Dad always let us water the garden."

"Really?" said Bear.

"Yes, **always**," said Caspar and Clive, winking at each other.

Caspar and Clive squirted the hose at Betsy and Bill.
Betsy and Bill threw a bucket of water at
Anna and Adelaide, and Anna and Adelaide
poured the watering can over Caspar and Clive.

Everyone was wet, cross and miserable.

"We shouldn't be playing this game!" wept Caspar and Clive.

"That Bear can't babysit.

That Bear is hopeless.

That Bear is . . .

. . . very busy! Bear, what are you doing?"

"Oh!" said Bear. "I'm building a ship. I'm going on an adventure."

"Wait!" said the bunnies. "Can we come, too?"

They helped Bear build an excellent ship
with room for everyone, even Dottie.

Then they set sail and forgot
to feel cold or cross.

They'd been exploring for nearly 27
whole minutes when Bear let down
the anchor and jumped ashore.

"Bear," said Betsy and Bill,
"where are you going?"

"All adventurers need something to eat," said Bear.

"Wait!" called the bunnies. "Can we come, too?"

They dug up rare rooty shapes. They picked pink things. They gathered heaps of crunchy leaves. The bunnies ate until their tummies were completely full, and no one felt sick at all.

And then it started to get dark.

"I can hear something in the trees," said Anna.

"It's the Bunny Beast," said Adelaide.

"We're scared!" cried the bunnies.
And they pulled their ears down over their eyes.

But Bear found an old book.

"Bear," said Anna and Adelaide,
"what are you reading?"

Bear smiled. "Once upon
a time," he said, "there
was a family of sleepy
little bunnies . . ."

One by one, the bunnies gathered around Bear.
And one by one, they fell fast asleep.

By the time Mr and Mrs Burrow came home, all the bunnies were tucked up in bed.

"Well, Bear!" said Mrs Burrow. "How are the bunnies?"

Bear smiled. "They are a delight," he said.

"Really?" asked Mr Burrow.

The bunnies peeped out from under their covers.

"Yes, always," said Bear, winking.

Mr and Mrs Burrow smiled as Bear shuffled home.

"Well," said Mrs Burrow.
"That Bear can babysit."

"Yes," said Mr Burrow.
"Six little bunnies, safe and sound."

Mrs Burrow gulped.
"Wait a minute," she said.
"Did you say **six**?"

"Seven little bunnies, safe and sound!

Night night, Dottie."